WALKING IN MY SHADOW

ACT PLAY IN MOTION

DOUG MCPHILLIPS

Also, by Doug McPhillips:

Other Visionary Stories:
NOVELS.
From Darkness to Light.
Awake to my Gutted Dream.
The Sword of Discernment.
Santiago Traveller.
I Prophet.
Master's at my table.
The Guru of Jerusalem.
We are upside down. (Biography)
The Wicklow Way.
The Adventures of Ace McDice.
Instant Karma & Grace.
The Credo.
Reflections of an Old Man.
Reincarnation of the Assassin
Masters of Introspection.
Journey to a hermit's haven.
The Rise and Rise of a 4th Reich
Grandad's tales are tall and true.
Into Action: Alcoholics for Jesus
Lightbulb Moments
For Pete's Sake
A Camino Guide Book.
Country Camino. (Album).
Santiago Traveller. (Album).
Soul Fact. (Album).

Doug McPhillips Circa 2025 ISBN. 978-1-7638868-5-8

National Library of Australia Catalogue-in-Publication data: New Holy Bible, International Version, Hodder & Stoughton, 1980. Alcoholics Anonymous, 4th Edition, AA World Service, 1976.

As Bill sees it, 8th Print, AA World Service. 2017

Daily Reflections, 11th Print, AA World Service 2014.

Journey to the Inner Mountain, Hodder & Staughton, James Cowan, 2002.

The Choice is always ours, Jove Publishing, 1997.

Santiago traveller, Ingram Spark, Doug McPhillips, 2018.

Chopping Wood, Short Run Press, David Bernz, 2023

Where have all the flowers gone? WW Norton & Co, 2006

How to play a string banjo. Peter Seeger, self-published,1962

The Times and Times of Bob Dylan: A Biography. Lulu Press, 2016.

Woody Guthrie- A Life- Joe Klein, Random House, 1999

Path to Self-Man and his Symbols- Carl Jung 1964.

Notebook Research.

Google research- Authors Unknown.

This book combines fact and fiction. All characters in this novel are either real or fictional, and the names of people living at the time may be genuine or invented. Any resemblance to actual events, places, or people, whether living or deceased, is purely coincidental; however, what is relevant is indeed real. When poetic licence alters fact into fiction, names have been changed to protect the innocent.

Contents:

Introduction

An older man, interviewed in his later years by the media, has built a legacy of literary and musical achievements that, on the surface, explore universal themes of love, loss, social injustice, and the human condition. At first, he responds to questions about his past and creative pursuits with openness, curiosity, humility, and good spirit. However, as the interview progresses, he becomes aware of a still, small voice within wanting to be heard above the noise of his egocentric answers and the applause of the studio audience. So, his responses become more careful, as being part of the world now is not his true wish. The story is told by someone who, after a period of conflict, has come to terms with their inner self and realises that they no longer seek worldly desires.

In consideration of the sensitivity of the place and time, the older man answers the interviewer's questions, for the sake of his audience and the mission to which he has agreed, with care and truth. He is wise to the course he has embarked upon, but ever mindful of the still, small voice that is within. The shadow self is crying for attention, and the pure creative child within is innocently listening to the dialogue as related to the elder self's version of events.

The story unfolds behind the layers of reality as the old man reexamines events connected to the questions asked of him. What his mind perceives is a dialogue between his shadow self and the pure innocence of the child, who must be reminded of what happened through the actual events of his life, while he attempts to make sense of it all as part of his duty to his audience but also to connect with his soul in exploring a new way of living in the modern world.

Cast a stone into water,
watched the wake trails fade,
Life is like that, a fading thing,
Watching the ripples,
as they lap upon the shore.

Cast my burden like a stone,
into the river of life...
watched the ripples as
They fade away upon the shore.

Feel the wind ripple the water,
like loves and dreams of the past,
The wake trails of water to shore,
It all just fades, and it dies.

Put down the book and the pencil,
leave the old guitar aside,
let go of the songs of the memories,
It's all wake trails to the shore.

Just fading memories of the past,
They do not last for long,
like wake trails to the water,
like wake trails to the shore.

Then, looking back on that path,
You may,
The footprints made are gone.
Like wake trails to the shore.

Pilgrim,
There is no other, there is no way,
Only wake trails to the water
Wake trail to the shore..
 fade away. fade away

WALKING IN MY SHADOW

A Play in Motion

ACT 1.

The Studio Interview

ACT 2.

Dialogue with the Shadow

ACT 3.

Rebirth of the Innocent

ACT 4.

Time to Consider

Cast of Characters

ALVIS: An octogenarian man, a golden ager, knowing the limits of his wisdom, gives counsel on his creative legacy.

KEIR: An inner shadow spirit of Alvis, who is the strength, resilience and loyalty that make up Alvis' inner character from the dark aspects of his spirit. He is highly emotional, driven by primal instincts, and often angry, concealed from the world by the conscious Alvis, but longs for control and expression, emerging from the dark into the light.

MANAK: The innocent child within Alvis, beyond Keir, displays kindness, affection, and is a pure soul. He is also the in-depth connection to the mind and intellect of the older man in his dotage.

NARRATOR: The voice of Keir within the mind of Alvis, who sometimes quietly seeks expression by speaking to the mind.

THE CHILD: Another voice inclined to express ideas through the imagination of Alvis, but with sights, cries, and mumbles.

ACT 1: THE STUDIO INTERVIEW

In a studio with an audience.

Alvis, the older man, sits in contemplation, sipping his first cup of coffee for the day. The initial mouthful of the dark nectar clears away the cobwebs of the night as he prepares himself for the upcoming interview with a well-known journalist famous for asking probing questions to his victims, driven by an inquisitive mind. Life has often been unkind to the octogenarian about to face the interview. Yet, he also believes that everything life has dealt him has been necessary lessons contributing to his perceived wisdom. As a result, he holds no regrets about his past and would gladly go through it all again, knowing that what has been achieved and lost along the way has been worthwhile in living life on its own terms.

In a previous life, Alvis has had numerous interviews about his creative works and reflects on the fact that he has experienced more than, as artist Andy Warhol put it, "In the future everyone will be famous for 15 minutes." He was early for the interview, as is his habit, and showed no sign of nerves; nor had he prepared for any questions that might come up. Believing now in the attitude that he would answer honestly and openly if he chose to answer, any questions asked of him.

He was already feeling the heat from the studio lights but had chosen to keep his dark glasses on, so the reflection from the light didn't bother him. Alvis looked around the studio as the audience slowly began to fill the stands, waiting for the popular interviewer to take the stage and start the show. He had time to take in the setting and watched as the teleprompter was set up behind him. It was clear to him that the interviewer had pre-set his questions and could switch to the prompter whenever he wished, rather than ad-libbing, so to speak. Alvis wondered if the audience was a fixed group who would respond with applause or laughter when prompted by signage. He saw no other promotional signs for the audience apart from the one for the TV personality, the well-known interviewer. Alvis felt pleased about this, as he preferred people to be spontaneous rather than artificial. The older man took a final look around the stage, noticing the only other item of interest — a chair for the interviewer. The rest of the stage was free of distractions, apart from a jug of water and two glasses on a small footstool beside the chairs. He was glad, as in many past interviews, that the TV personality sat behind a desk, which to him seemed like a barrier, creating a divide between the interviewee and the one asking questions.

A make-up artist stepped out from behind a screen to pat his face with a powder puff and put on a bit of makeup. Alvis waved her away, preferring to stay as natural as God made him. He was never one to let his appearance be more than what nature provided. He had shrunk slightly with age, looked world-weary, and was a bit wrinkled around the eyes. He seemed fit and healthy, aside from a slight pot belly, which he figured was acceptable for a man his age and size. The crowd began to cheer loudly as the well-dressed interviewer with a spring in his step entered stage left to greet his next subject. Then the hush was absolute as the interviewee shook hands with Alvis. He now felt like he was lining up for the first round of a professional boxing match, faintly recalling his one bout against a champion who had won nine professional titles. Alvin had fought the pro for three rounds and managed a draw, but deep down, he knew who actually won. The professional ended up without a mark, while Alvis left with a split lip and two black eyes. He quickly shoved aside that memory, reminding himself not to get caught out by the interviewer's punch-like questions.

The interviewer started his introduction by branding his "victim" with a title: "Welcome to this night of nights with the infamous Alvin." The interviewer had, without any salutation, cast dispersions upon his guest by branding him "infamous' without any justification, upon which Keir, the dark shadow self, only grunted within the mind of the interviewee. Alvin, always the entrepreneur, files the 'infamous Alvin' away to use in a future promotion of one of his books or songs. The crowd clapped without needing to be prompted.

Smiling with a grim-like grin, the interviewer, pleasantly enough, spoke about nothing in particular, offered Alvis a glass of water, which he graciously accepted. He poured one for himself, took a sip as did Alvis, and, unlike his guest, appeared quite nervous and perspired profusely under the stage lights. Without any further ado, the interviewer began a barrage of questions, trying to get to the heart of what made up this legendary older man. Alvis answered, deflecting the questions like a seasoned footballer dodging a tackle, and spoke in short sentences when necessary, often monosyllables. The interviewer appeared uneasy, failing to achieve what he had set out to do, as he tried to break down his subject in front of the TV cameras and studio audience. Alvis took pity on his opponent and attempted to answer the probing questions with a bit more detail where he thought it appropriate.

Interviewer: "So, Alvis, unlike the majority of humanity, you have achieved a level of fame by the volume of your output in stories and songs. Would you call your success a rich legacy of artistic talent, or are you just another hack writer who struck it lucky?" A note of sarcasm was in his question, and whilst Alvis was being prompted by the inner emotional voice of Keir, his shadow self, he replied with care and truthfulness.

Alvis: "Whilst some may think that the majority of my work is limited to commercial pieces, I tend to write whatever comes to mind, which is why I have books in many different genres."

Interviewer: "It seems like now there are so many people who have written stories like you do, but get little payment for their effort. Do you write for fame or fortune?"

Alvis: "Neither, I write that someone may get some personal benefit out of what I write."

Interviewer: "So what of the great legacy that is perceived you have in your volumes of words?

Alvis: "It matters little, for whilst one may achieve an element of fame after one's demise, we all soon fade into oblivion in time. It is all just a whiff of smoke in the scheme of things."

The interviewer, who has yet to discover what motivates Alvis, tries a different approach. He assumes there are other reasons why the author and songwriter chose the path of creativity later in life rather than in his youth.

Interviewer: "So, Alvis, in my research, I noticed that you have only started writing books and recording songs in the past decade. What did you do for a living before you turned to creativity?"

Alvis was now being prompted by his shadow self, longing for expression. Keir, in his narrative voice, wanted to be heard to say: 'I was once a banker, an engineer's assistant, a salesman and a manager, a wholesaler, a retailer, king maker and political scout," but instead Alvis, much to the disgust of his alter ego Keir, responded: " I've been a jack of all trades."

Alvis bore no ill will towards the interviewer and wasn't aiming to dominate the verbal exchange or boost his own profile; his aim was simply to encourage the studio and TV viewers to consider his books and songs for their own benefit, nothing more. The interviewer soon ran out of questions about the author's past. So, he shifted to showing a montage of Alvis's books on screen, reflecting on the synopsis of each as they might appeal, thereby encouraging questions from the audience while he gathered his thoughts.

Interviewer, being a little more lenient now, enquired: "What set you off on the Camino pilgrimages, and what has transpired as a consequence?"

Then, within Alvis, he heard Keir's voice reminding him of his three Camino pilgrimages and how they had been a catalyst for his recovery from anxiety and depression. Keir wanted to speak about how he had ventured out the first time to overcome the pain and loss of his family, his business, and to some degree his sanity after a son's suicide. Alvis, mindful of Keir's eccentricity, preferred a more subdued analysis of his Caminos, highlighting the first pilgrimage and recounting his second journey; the latter had been more about seeking a love interest than spiritual redemption. He had often chased after Tinker Bell like Peter Pan, instead of settling for the stability of Wendy. He had travelled to Never Never Land more often than not, not before he resigned himself to friendship over lustful desires. He felt it best to include all three journeys in one telling of the third, relating it to his Camino book, and reflecting on the first and second journeys. It was more important to him that the audience understood the message of buying the book or at least recognised the benefits of walking the Camino for their own reasons. He smiled to himself, pleased that the past Camino journeys had been met with applause from the studio audience. As an afterthought regarding love and his past Camino efforts, he said to the audience in a logical way, "We chase after the love of a woman instead of turning to God."

Alvis, unwilling to let Keir's voice dominate his expression of egocentricity, was taken aback by Manuk's awakening, who found his voice above the echo of the ego that always seemed to overshadow his innate, natural childlike self. The voice first emerged as a strained sound that gurgled up into Alvis' throat, nearly choking him as he tried to keep it barely audible. The pure, childlike expression surfaced above the noise of Keir's voice, sounding like a cry from deep within the older man. Alvis fought back tears that welled in his eyes. He masked them by wiping his eyes and brow, pretending he was affected by the heat of the studio lights, feigning discomfort. He reached for the glass beside him on the table and took a small sip of water. Maintaining his composure, under the influence of his pure child, Manuk—now free to express his feelings—spoke honestly of his Camino experiences.

Manuk on his Camino.

Manuk, the pure child inside, had been suppressed for most of the older man's life. Alvis remembered how he created an imaginary self to cope with losing a blood brother when he was young, instead of letting Manuk, the innocent child within, suffer life's hardships. He thought at the time that adopting a new identity was the best move, as he, Alvis, could follow his instincts. The egocentric Keir, feeling false love, preferred to live a life of deception rather than face the tough realities of a well-lived life. It worked for quite a while, as he learned to bury his feelings instead of confronting the pain and the spiritual work that comes with trusting the pure child of love inside.

The inward journey took a toll on him throughout his life. Alvis avoided facing harsh truths, numbing his feelings with pleasure, material pursuits, and an unrelenting craving for applause to satisfy Keir, his alter ego. It worked most of the time, but deep down, he never found happiness in the feelings he chased. Every time life threw him a curveball, he would laugh it off, seeking more enjoyable experiences. When struck by a minor blow, like a bike crash, he suffered little; similarly, when hit with force comparable to a motor vehicle, he would drown his pain in drink. Eventually, he couldn't take the impact of painful events any longer. It was only after losing everything—his wife, family, business, and a son—by his own hand that he fell into total ruin, sank into severe depression, and, seeking help, turned to a higher power for spiritual guidance. The answers came during a pilgrimage to Santiago de Compostela—The Way of Saint James, the Apostle of Christ.

Alvis chose to channel his creativity to support the child who had suffered silently deep within his soul. The interviewer inquired about his Camino experiences and their influence. He sat quietly for some time, reflecting on the most meaningful events that had triggered the changes guiding his Camino journey, while also inspiring a lotus flower of creative ideas he felt compelled to uncover within himself. He knew he needed to be careful to nurture the spirit of the innocent child inside. The world does not need to know the depth of love that was planted—like the seed of life he felt within. Instead, he could openly share his innermost love with the world. He realised that the Way was no longer about worldly pursuits. Such a path was the vain, glorious chase of the linear, logical mind, rooted in materialism.

He knew he had found a pearl of great price—something spiritual that couldn't be expressed through worldly values. Now he was walking the middle road, the path of the spirit that the world had yet to grasp. No matter how much Keir protested, it was the Manuk child's pure expression that was needed now. Alvis had resigned himself to the belief that he was a square peg trying to fit into a round hole. It was inevitable that he would turn inward to the spirit within for guidance. Wisdom had come from experience, and he understood that he must live in this world, if not of it. It was still vital for him to express himself through writing and song, but for reasons entirely different from what the world might understand. So, Alvis allowed the Manuk child to express his feelings and creativity. Whilst Alvis recognised that his power came from the Universal creator, he nonetheless had expectations of the child's creativity within. He began to play a repetitive tune on his guitar. He didn't know what would emerge from the Manuk child. Suddenly, he felt his voice burst into song. It was as if the child within knew how to bring a sense of closure to the interviewer. He did not know what would emerge from the child's self-questioning, only that he related to the reasons for walking the Camino Way. The song catalysed understanding of the journey's meaning, and it provided closure.

Walking along, Alvis continued to strum his guitar, finding chords that seemed to fit the child's voice.

Singing my song, Alvis was getting into it now.

Here in my heart, [four beats to each note]

Santiago!

Starry eyes,
clear blue skies,
heading for joy,
Santiago!

There's no point,
turning back where,
Look straight ahead,
along the track there.

Walking to Santiago.

Travelled far,
calling for love,
cobblestone path too,
Santiago!

Release pain,
Put down your pack,
You're almost home,
Santiago!

Walking to Santiago.

Darkness gone,
tears of joy,
seeing the light,
Santiago!

Milky Way,
guiding my path,
You're almost home,
Santiago!

There's no point,
turning back where,
Look straight ahead,
along the track there.

Walking to Santiago.

Dawning light,
guiding my feet,
beat of my heart,
Santiago!

Darkness gone,
bright sunny days,
living the life,
Santiago!

The interviewer summarised the old man's Camino mission: "Alvis walked the epic 800 km Camino de Santiago not once but three times. His pilgrimages have been in response to the tragedies and hardships he has personally faced, and he credits the Camino for changing his perspective on life." The interview encouraged the audience to take a short break, and as the stage curtain closed.

ACT 2: DIALOGUE WITH THE SHADOW

Stage and Screen.

Alvis sat in the darkness of the stage, the only light being the screen behind him, which still displayed the book page of his website. He was well pleased.. The scene was set on a deserted beach projected on the screen, which reappeared as the stage curtain was pulled back, with background drops visible behind the studio. Alvis and the Interviewer come into view in the foreground, along with the studio audience. Keir, the narrator, describes the journey unfolding through Alvis as seen through his eccentric alter ego, his shadow self. He sees the story as the scenery shifts like a film at his whim.

The waves crash violently onto the shore, reflecting the turmoil inside. For it's I, Keir; my chance to bother the tireless master, Alvis. It is I, Keir, walking along the seashore. Alvis is just a young boy in his preteens, nervously pondering the meaning of life. What made him feel different from those around me? Why could he not love as others appeared to? Keir, in his undoubtedly egocentric way, seemed to encourage the sad Alvis to stay apart from the chaotic crowd, preferring solitude over company. Keir, while struggling with Alvis's inquisitive mind, had long ago taken control over Manuk, the innocent child inside, creating a deception to avoid pain and suffering, for Keir had unwittingly led the creative child and Alvis, the logical, linear part of the young boy, into adopting his viewpoint of life.

Oh, I am now alone, Alvis thought. Why is it so? In his egocentric nature, Keir participates in team sports, and I did communicate effectively with childhood friends. Keir had fun playing games, chasing girls, pulling their hair, or hiding in the schoolyard, daring to kiss a girl who took his fancy, though he was the captive of his emotions. Alvis always completed his schoolwork and made a reasonable effort to earn good reports each term. Yet, he seemed to lack the chance to fulfil the egocentric part of his destiny. On this deserted beach, Alvis feels alone. He recognises himself alone with only the sand crabs at his feet for company. He sinks his feet into the sand as he walks.

The waves continued their rhythmic crashing onto the shore, creating foam at the edge, then retreated only to crash against the beach again and again. What are these waves saying as I walk? Keir, within the young boy replies, " Death! Death! Death! " Alvis hears but chooses to ignore, for there is little that this alter ego has accomplished, little done to be recognised so that He may be loved. So Alvis shouted over the sound of death's toll. He shouted aloud, " Live! Live! Live!' Like a flickering candle in the wind, I must keep the flame alive, forevermore."

Keir, now in full flight, begins to recount his exploits... Recount the start of the Camino story to give the audience a sense of his egocentric experience, while also acknowledging the reasons for undertaking this pilgrimage. He has condensed the three Caminos into one story with the clear aim of promoting Alvis's book and songs from his Camino album. He starts just as it happens: "It's not just a walk in the woods; the Camino Way, also known as the Napoleon route, begins at St. Jean in the foothills of the Pyrenees and finishes 800 kilometres away in Santiago, Spain. Over hill and dale, from rugged mountains to valley floors, desert plains, through ancient villages and historic city cobblestone streets. It's not for the faint-hearted, the constant daily grind of your Camino. Bone weariness, injury or illness, and a sense of being alone with your head and heart are constant companions. Fellow pilgrims who lit The Way were complete strangers who created a bond of friendship, greeting each other with "Buen Camino," meaning "good journey."

Keir had looked around the audience to see how much the studio audience was paying attention to his dialogue. Content that he had them in his full grasp, he continued….

"The pilgrimage is not just an outward journey; the long inward track of The Way is both a dream and a reality. It's a daily reminder that one needs very little of the material world to be happy. Fellow pilgrims may be on a journey seeking a new vision, inner spiritual guidance, or to figure something out, to heal, or simply to take a long walk. Pilgrims have walked The Way for over 1000 years, following the Way of St. James, the apostle of Christ. Some believe his bones lie under the altar at the Cathedral in Santiago, where the traditional way finishes with a Christian celebration. Whatever the reasons for undertaking the Camino, whether as a believer or non-believer, it's a long walk, one that moves the body, mind, and spirit from place to place. A chance to be apart, to breathe in a holy work, to encounter, to glimpse the mystery.

Typical of Keir, he never shies away from seeking recognition for what Alvis has contributed. Now, he is taking credit for his pilgrimage works, the author's books, and his songs. "The essence of this story is a promotion for the author of the book and album songs 'Santiago Traveller', but it's not mandatory to consume both." Keir proudly accepts the applause of the crowd, while secretly,

Alvis regrets letting him out of his cage, so to speak, because he had been more content lately, having escaped the applause, the chaotic crowd, and the lure of materialism. He makes a mental note to be more cautious about his egocentric tendencies in the future. A certain ego is necessary, but it should be just a small speck on the beach in the grand scheme. For once, Keir, the shadow self, believes himself to be the whole beach, and that is where the danger lies.

Alvis, pondering Keir's wild and mad ways, reflected on how Keir's falsehood had driven him onto a reckless charger during his first Camino pilgrimage. It wasn't only after returning home that Keir had persuaded Alvis to hand over control to him during his Camino journeys. The risk of death was what Keir had as his ultimate goal, and it would happen multiple times in future travels. It would take time before Alvis learnt to take ownership of his shadow self's tendencies to dominate. Alvis understood that, despite his good intentions, he would fail many times before grasping the wisdom of being in the present moment within his Higher Self, and surrendering that spiritual part that overcomes the shadow. He began to recall one of the many episodes from his first Camino, where Keir had stealthily approached him and taken over his better nature for his spirit.

The Mad Campaigner.

Alvis was reconsidering the events in his past life that he had allowed Keir to take control over his better nature. He cast his mind back to a particular day on the first of his Camino pilgrimages.

Alvis was climbing higher now, up the steepest ridge of the Pyrenees mountains. He felt quite pleased with himself, having shed many dark shadows of painful events in his life. The day was bright and clear, and the sun was low in the late afternoon, so the forty-two-degree heat had cooled somewhat. As he rounded a ridge, he noticed a long-legged female walker striding out at a faster pace than his own. She had that look about her of someone who had climbed the highest peaks in a past life, and Keir wasn't going to let her out-stride him. It was typical of when Keir, his competitive shadow self, would lift himself up to rattle Alvis's logical brain and get fully involved. While Alvis was aware of the long-legged female's presence, who seemed unfazed by the older man walking nearby, he noticed she was more athletic than he was —tall and strong in a typical German manner, whereas he was shorter and stockier. Always the competitor, Alvis had Keir pulling the strings within his mind, boosting his pace. He knew he had an edge because he was using walking poles, which gave him extra support to keep ahead of the woman closing in on his heels. Keir was in his element, pushing Alvis to work harder. Eventually, the German athlete slowed a little and called out as Alvis pulled ahead: "What's the rush?" she cried. Keir, the shadow self, put a smile on Alvis's face, recognising that the woman was a competitive spirit too.

That evening, the German female athlete and two Austrian male pilgrims sat with Alvis over a pilgrims' meal, discussing the day's events. The German woman soon pointed out what had happened on the mountain when she tried to pass Alvis. She was surprised that the short, determined Australian had outpaced her. " He is mad," she said. Both Austrians who had walked with Alvis the day before agreed completely. Alvis responded, "How do you know I'm mad?"

The Austrian replied: "Well, I know because I rode a pushbike over 10,000 kilometres around Australia and across the desert a couple of years back. To do that, I must be mad too. " The other recounted other events that endorse a kind of madness in each of them, including walking the Camino. They all raise their glasses in toast: "To some kind of madness."

Alvis refocused his thoughts on the present and realised he still had plenty of time to think before the final part of his interview. He reflected on the influences that had pushed him from being a logical, straightforward, clear-thinking person to a madman at times in the past. More often than not, it was when he was drunk that his conscious mind was clouded by alcohol, allowing the shadow self to take over completely, even leading to dangerous actions. He recalled instances of playing chicken in cars, riding recklessly on a wing and a prayer, being chased by a policeman on a motorcycle while intoxicated, and surviving spectacular car crashes unscathed. He remembered an event from his wild youth when he took a cruise on a small Russian passenger liner.

A cyclonic storm mindset.

The Russian cruise ship was normally set to travel from Tokyo, Japan, to Vladivostok, Russia—the connection to the Trans-Siberian railway for those trading with the so-called free world. However, this time, it was on a short trip to carry passengers from Perth in Western Australia to Singapore. The Siberian rail link was temporarily shut at that time, and it was snowed in.

Alvis had secured cheap passage on a trip to London via Singapore, first by ship and then a charter flight from Singapore onward to his ultimate destination. As it happened, both the ship journey and the flight proved hazardous, but he felt the need to recall the ship journey and the experience he had on board only now. The ship was small, a rustic vessel that badly needed a coat of paint and some wire-brush treatment for areas of rust that could be seen wherever one looked. He had made his way down the galley way to a cabin at the bow on the starboard side. There were no beds, just three hammocks slung sideways to go with the sway of the ship fore and aft. Alvis threw his knapsack onto one hammock and made his way back on deck to watch the shoreline as it slowly disappeared on the horizon.

A quick tour of the ship revealed a small bar, kitchen and dining area next door, and a staircase that led to the lower accommodation. He had ascertained that there could not have been more than 300 passengers on board, including the Russian crew.

Soon enough, Alvis was acquainted with his fellow roommates, two young men from Perth. They soon headed for the upstairs bar before dinner, which included a beef stroganoff and side dishes like potatoes and pasta. This meal didn't vary much during the week on board, except for the occasional lunch meal, which included fish or meat. The chef always loaded a side plate with a large helping of caviar. Breakfast was always the same, with porridge and cold meat dishes. It was funny how, after all these years, he could still remember what he ate, yet when it came to the excessive drinking, he had no idea what he had consumed on that hazardous journey.

The Russian captain and navigator, having no idea about the rough weather in the Indian Ocean, probably read a storm warning from the coast guard incorrectly and, after just one day at sea, changed course and headed straight into a full-blown cyclone. The small ship creaked and shuddered with every blow of the massive waves. First, the waves would hit twice head-on, then broadside along either one side or the other of the ship, causing more noise and shudder as the boat bobbed like a cork in a bathtub of water.

There was no way to get proper rest in the sleeping quarters, so the brave travelling mates and one other, a Dutch photographer, spent the entire trip clinging to the bar and our drinks while riding out the sea swells. They did not see another passenger on that voyage, except for a brief day when the ship entered the calm eye of the storm around the reef. In some cases, passengers, green around the gills, made it on deck. Their appearance was short-lived, as the ship soon returned to the cyclone.

Now, here's the thing. Alvis was quite happy to have a drink with his mates, waiting for the journey to Singapore to end. It was when the Captain announced over the intercom that the trip would be rough over the next few days, and he had ordered his crew to batten down all the hatches and lock the deck doors. It was at that point that Alvis gave in to temptation and took a risk after drinking quite a bit. The shadow side of Keil always wants to tempt fate, choosing death over life, and was listening to the voice of the Dutch photographer. He had an idea to climb the mast and snap a photo of the bow as it disappeared into an oncoming wave. So, the wise Alvis was later overwhelmed by the thrill-seeking Keil within and volunteered to join him.

It was no issue to unwind the hatch door to make their way on deck. They locked the hatch behind them as they moved along the deck toward the bow and the maskhead, all the while holding onto an inner rail for support. At one point, they were climbing upward as the ship rose on a wave, and the next, they faced downhill on the other side of the wave. Before the ship had time to broadside into another wave, the photograph and Alvis were halfway up the masthead. They hadn't reached the top when the boat went into a head-on wave. The forward deck vanished into the wave as it engulfed it. The photographer quickly snapped a photo and held on, and Alvis, now clear-headed, sober as a judge, was almost washed overboard by the water's impact that overwhelmed them. Without hesitation, as the wave subsided, they made their way back along the deck, undid the hatch, and headed for the bar for a strong drink to settle the adrenaline rush. It was a foolish thing to do, but that was typical of what Alvis fell for when he let his Keir spirit take the reins.

Keir, the shadow self, is always on a mission to tempt Alvis, from his better self, toward danger and possible death. It seemed to Alvis that human nature was the lure leading him to be attracted to all that was unpure. The biblical text revealed this, and history has repeated it through wars, trouble, and strife, with many men choosing death over life.

Alvis, at his lowest point, surely considered the alternative of ending his own life, as life had left him in a precarious position. He had weighed all options. The Way of man seemed to be the right path for a time, but he soon realised in his adulthood that the material world proved fruitless and he was made of sterner stuff. He was more determined than ever to keep the flame alive, flickering within him. While he had breath to breathe, he would use his God-given talents to pursue what gives life meaning over death.

Alvis had read the works of many wise men who seemed to know the in-depth of life experience, and yet so many of them had come to grief and chose death rather than have the courage to face life on life's terms. He had concluded that they likely gave lip service to love but did not truly love or give themselves to others. To Alvis, this was the key to his faith that he clung to even in moments of despair, for it took him a long time to come to love.

ACT 3: THE REBIRTH OF AN INNOCENT

The remaking of a child.

Meanwhile, Manak, the innocent child within Alvis, that pure soul who displays kindness, affection, and a deep connection to Alvis's mind and intellect in his dotage, was now biding his time for attention again.. He is the one, aside from his brief appearance, to sing his 'Santiago' song to the audience, embodying Alvis's innocence—a part of him that the old man often forgets but is ever-present. He patiently waits for his turn to shine, for he can see through Alvis's mind's eye that he has been ignored for so long and is now coming of age. The older man realises that he must let Manak express himself through creative outpouring, and he must also tell his own story. Alvis returns to the present as the studio lights brighten and the movie screen returns to blankness. Alvis files the introspective thought away for another time, for he does not see the need to share it with the interviewer or the studio audience at the moment. He is happy to let his egocentric self hold court, so to speak, until he can exhaust this shadow while walking in it a little longer.

Murak, the pure child of creative love, had been left with his Alvis self, feeling alone and abandoned as a child. It was the fault, if you will, of the mother lode, the one who had abandoned the child at birth. It was not entirely her fault, for she had suffered much from postnatal depression that never left her. It seemed right for her to leave Alvis with loneliness and abandonment in a cage-like structure for safety and protection in her mind. Thus, it came to pass that as a small boy, he was only picked up and adored when an audience arrived to see the child. It was then that the mother lode encouraged Alvis to take the stage. Then and there, the shadow self took control, for each of those inner personalities was conditioned into thinking that love was given in applause when performing. Keil, the shadow self, had lied to the Murak, and being of innocence, he believed the dark soul. It took a long while for Alvis to come to terms with his demon self and embrace the child within. For he achieved fame and fortune in his adult life as a mask for love and affection. Finding ultimately that all is an empty retreat into despair, depression, and anxiety, when his world comes crashing down.

As the interviewer set the stage for another barrage of questions, Alvis retreated into past thoughts of his excessive drinking brought on more by his life's goals and love turning pear-shaped, which led him to a stint in rehabilitation to dry out and make some sense of his life. The first hospitalisation was more driven by despair for the loss of all his life seemed at the time to stand for. He did some therapy there, but it proved of little worth. The psychotherapist prescribed some heavy, addictive medications, which ultimately proved to be of little benefit to his mental state. The upside was that through a fellow patient, he made contact with the fellowship of Alcoholics Anonymous, which led him to follow a spiritual path of letting go of whatever came up on any given day.

Alvis, until that moment, felt a sense of separation from God. He believed that nature and the animal kingdom, like eagles and crows, provided signs of the dark side gaining control over his life. He thought he needed a prototype of his conception, so he mistakenly believed and embraced the body of a woman as a substitute for God. The desire for lustful satisfaction overruled his better nature for a time. It brought him to more grief than he could have ever imagined, but ultimately, he found his way clear to walk the Camino de Santiago for the first time. The depth of his night of the soul has led him to enter the dragon's mouth of fear. There, he found the dragon transform into a lotus flower of creative ideas, resulting in the success of his Camino books and songs upon his return home. He had then once more returned to the Camino in search of love, but all he found was pain and loss again. It landed him back in rehabilitation for a time. There, he realised he didn't know himself at all. It was the Keir that he knew, and the child self had been buried beneath the pain and suffering of living life falsely. Murak, the child, was now ready to emerge and be exposed.

This time, the older man returned to the Camino, let go of his burdens, and stopped taking his medications cold turkey. He returned to the Camino for himself, not for another.

Alvis was making his way along the last tired stretch of the road to Santiago. He was reminiscing about the last spring wildflowers he saw near Lisbon on his previous Camino. His connection with nature and humanity was evident in a sacred grove of stones. He remembered standing among massive granite stones, feeling as if he was in a crowded group of granite friends jostling to catch a glimpse. The brave adventurer depicted the transition of the itinerant hunter-gatherers to farming around 5000 BC, when scientific evidence suggests these stones were erected. What made its astronomical alignments even clearer was the presence of two large stones marking the summer and winter solstices. At the spring and autumn equinoxes, both the sun and the moon rise at the same point along the axis of the stones, providing a perfect way for early crop growers to determine when to sow and harvest. Nearby graves contained human bones and hunting and agricultural implements, testifying to the human spirit of that distant past. It seemed like they had a human sacrifice to the Gods or paid homage by burying their dead at the site. The symbolic stones were not only an astronomical guidance method to the tribe's survival but also a modern-day reminder of their very existence.

 As Alvis reflected on this during his second Camino, now walking the French route again, he was reminded of the news in the local papers before leaving home about an Indigenous rock shelter near Kakadu that pushes Australian human history back 65,000 years, up to 18,000 years earlier than any archaeologists previously believed. Alvis's homeland, steeped in ancient wisdom and this sacred land on the Iberian Peninsula, with a history even bloodier than his own, spoke to him of savagery, poverty, power, prestige, conquest, social uprising, defeat, and heroism. Endless cycles of action and reaction persist to this day.

Alvis walked The Way along a sandy track, his mind drifting back once more to that time with a Portuguese lover, the lunch they enjoyed together, and their hand-in-hand walk along a nudist beach. He remembered being the only person dressed. The Goddess of his dreams had squeezed his hand tenderly, kissed his cheek affectionately, and turned her blue eyes to his, saying in English, "I think I love you." If she had spoken in any other of the many languages she knew, he would still have understood, despite not speaking any of them. The language of love lingered for a moment, and he briefly believed her passionate words. There in Portugal, the sun burned, the flowers failed to bear fruit, leaves fell from dry, withered stems, and there was hardship in the land. Alvis's passion was intense, but he had long since realised that it was not love, just physical lust—a misconception, a shadow of love, a myth.

Back home in Australia, Alvis pictured the swamp oak trees of the Aboriginal songlines sighing incessantly, hungering for rain, the gum trees shedding tears of blood and turning into red gum. Bleeding as Christ had done in the Garden of Gethsemane, turning into dry blood on that Sacred face, his blue eyes tortured for what he could foresee—the future folly of humanity, wars and sufferings ahead, and his own physical passion for a foreign maiden. He couldn't see it then, as he walked his second Camino. He couldn't see it as he walked this third Camino, looking back on the first and the second. As Alvis writes these lines, He sees it now—the sad conclusion of the hopes of the Aboriginal peoples, the hopes of the world today, black or white, the folly of an old Camino man, walking in a strange land, looking to the sky and thinking of his homeland of the Southern Cross and all of humanity's beginnings in Africa. "We are all descendants of the Dreaming, whether we are black, white, or brindle," he heard himself saying.

So, after Alvis shared his perspective on life through his logical mind and this pilgrimage on The Camino, Keir's egocentric story about the Camino and his promotion of his books and album had led to some conclusions for the studio audience. It was Alvis who stepped forward and said: "My life's journey of striving and achieving long-held beliefs and goals, after many battles and hardships, did not bring feelings of contentment, fulfilment, or peace. The opposite happened, and for a long time, I couldn't understand why, having climbed to the top of the mountain, the view seemed grey, bleak, and empty. The belief that we need to have something or someone to win, gain a position of worldly power or responsibility, or acquire material possessions reveals a shallowness that often only becomes clear after being on the wrong path for too long, reaching the end, and realising it's just another crossroads. It's not the prize for the human heart; it's the struggle that makes us feel more alive, and it's to this that we offer our greatest love and commitment. And although we may be hesitant to admit it, it's the struggle that brings out the best in us."

Alvin finished his statement to the audience. He put down his guitar and decided not to sing another song for now. In retrospect, Alvis realised that all highly motivated people, like himself, risk inner defeat, which occurs when the prize has been won and life no longer feels meaningful. It's then that we embark on a Camino-like journey to find new purpose. To renew our commitment to life and rediscover that sense of future potential, a new goal must surpass our aspirations, providing a compelling motivation for what we have previously achieved. First, we need to achieve personal ambitions, and once these are met, a realisation of belonging to a larger community dawns. It's then that we refine our goals to make some contribution to the greater whole, allowing life to flow within us once again.

It was then that Alvis sat once more in the studio chair and reflected on the meaning of his journey along The Way, for Alvis had newfound goals and a quest for belief, which had been highlighted by his investigation of myth, legend, and folklore on his three Caminos. Having won some of his battles, discovered part of his true nature, and now seeming to find peace, but at the cost of exhaustion of body, mind, and spirit. Alvis, having allowed his shadow self to tell its side of the story, thought it worthwhile to cast his mind across the journeys and revisit The Way, like a spirit traveller hovering over the journey and reliving it.

The stage was set for the interviewer to ask more about his guests' Camino journeys. Alvis knew it was far wiser to keep his answer on topic without giving too much away about himself.

Interviewer: " You have shared about the route and your reasons for your adventure. In your view, what is the historical significance of the Camino?"

Alvis: " The influence and experience of the hunter-gatherers' conversion to community and village life over the centuries, the myths that developed since the time of Christ, which are still believed throughout Northern Spain today in small, insular hamlets. The still, existing influence of the occult, witchcraft and Christianity. The variety of architecture that exists throughout Celebration, like ' The running of the Bulls' and the link with the killing of saints. The link with Christ and St. James in Spain, the arts, music and economic changes influenced me on my journeys, which I have documented in my story of the Way in my writings."

Interviewer: " What did you discover about yourself and others on the Camino?"

Alvis: " I discovered a new sense of freedom, and that's what I thought I needed from a material perspective was not essential in reality. 'Less is more' so to speak, although in truth I still don't live that way, but I am conscious of the fact that in a changing world, materialism is a whiff of smoke in the scheme of things." Alvis hesitated, took a small mouthful of water from the glass and continued: " I come to believe that other needs are more important than my own... It's not all about Alvis anymore."

Interviewer: "You've written lots of books and songs, initially motivated by your Camino experiences. What do you hope listeners and readers will learn from your words and music? "

Alvis, consider this question for a moment before responding. He had concluded that if people were interested in his books or music, he need not sell them the idea. "There's something about that walk that draws you back - it inspires creativity. It's a real journey of awakening and enlightenment. What seems important in our three-dimensional world doesn't seem important when you're walking the Camino. There's a sense of freedom that you don't normally find in the modern world. I'm not necessarily suggesting people do the actual Camino de Santiago, but to step out there and do something different, to think about where they're at, and how their life is. That is what my books and songs are about."

Interviewer: " Why would you encourage others to complete their pilgrimage? "

Alvis: " I believe all people should get away from the known and step out into the unknown at some point in their lives. As stated by Phil Couineau: 'The traveller, the pilgrim cannot find deep meaning in their journey of life until they encounter what is truly sacred.' In truth, I see the doorway, but I am still climbing the mountain in that regard. Perhaps another Camino, what do you reckon?"

The interview seemed to be content with the proceedings and wound up this segment of the show with a ' thank you' to his guest, mindful only of the outer man, for he knew nothing of Keir, the shadowed self. Nor did he know of Murak, the child yet to emerge, who loved others but was so far only in the stories of Alvis, the writer.

Alvis shook hands with the interviewer and noted that the screen was still displaying his book page on his website. He decided to linger a while longer on stage, recounting in his mind the content of the interview and considering how he might make the most of his time in the studio before the final parting. The audience was making their way out, and the theatre was soon empty. He looked at the programme and realised that it would be at least another hour of interview time before the audience would vacate the premises. He considered how best to utilise the interval time, for it was pleasant enough to remain in the chair, watching the activity of the stagehands as they swept the floor and replaced the water jug with a fresh supply of water. The last thing they had overlooked was turning off the big screen, where he might gain some free publicity from the television audience as it displayed the book page of his website. How could he benefit from this break in proceedings in the studio? He started to think about his creative self.

It was Murak, the pure inner child, who came to mind, he who had a brief opportunity to shine his thoughts and feelings upon the world, but he had somehow realised from the moment of his conception that he was abandoned. Alvis knew that the child was just a psychological concept representing the childlike aspects of his personality and emotional state, the links to early childhood experiences and trauma. He knew, like Keil, that the shadow self, Murak, was not a literal child within, but rather a metaphor for the younger, more vulnerable parts of his being that were now influencing his adult thoughts, feelings, and behaviours.

In his attempt to consider Murak now, he cast his mind back to those early years when he, like the mother lode, had abandoned his Murak child. What was it that he remembered about the child? He had certainly tapped into its source of creative thoughts and feelings in his writings, but he knew that he needed to make some headway in his acknowledgement now, to encourage the child to take the stage and express himself through this older self. It was those early memories that he returned to. He said to himself, "'I must schedule more time to connect with the essence of myself that has crept out now for expression." Alvis made up his mind to recall the events that had influenced the young Murak, to give expression now to the emotions that were welling up inside him.

Alvis had returned from the first Camino with a renewed zest for life. He hadn't realised he was being driven by his desire to re-establish himself in the material world. He was worried that time was slipping away too fast. He longed to compensate for lost love, status, and wealth. At first, this seemed like his main focus, but the child within had discovered its creative purpose, and despite Keir's efforts to control Alvis, he could no longer suppress the child's creativity. So, he appeared to his logical mind and ego, believing he could achieve everything he wished for. Alvis remembered a biblical passage about Christ, who went into the desert to spend time with his God self, and was tempted by Satan to accept his offer that he could have all he desired if he worshipped him. Jesus rejected the evil spirit of Satan with the words: "Away with the Satan, for it is written, thou shalt not tempt the Lord thy God." Unfortunately for Alvis, he had tricked himself into thinking his egocentric shadow, which praised his ability to accomplish many things—including giving Murak, his child self, free rein in his choices—was his true self. His darker spirit's shadow hoped to lead him to despair and snuff out his flame, aiming to push him towards his downfall.

Alvis was now recalling his former state before venturing forth on the Camino for the first time. He had come unstuck through the past, shaped by the consequences of the trials that had befallen him.

An interview within an interview.

Alvis was seated, waiting for the interviewer and the audience to return, and now he was thinking about his past counselling sessions with Joe, the physiotherapist, before he had ever walked The Way of St. James to Santiago. He was now listening in his mind to the conversation he had with Joe more than a decade ago.

Joe: " We have had quite a few sessions now, Alvis and I need to do further evaluation of your progress to date. So I want you to close your eyes and cast your mind back to the most disturbing moment in your youth and tell me about it?"

Alvis: " I was just a small boy of maybe five. It was a late winter Saturday afternoon, almost dusk. I was out in the front garden with my mother as she tended to raking up the fallen leaves from the winter-weathered flower beds, sweeping the front gutters. The street lights had come on, beaming a pale purple glow. Looking over my shoulder, I could see the closed door of the room beyond the verandah where my blood brother John had died just one week prior. My mother was undoubtedly suffering and paid little attention to me. I was feeling all alone in the world. That is when I closed off the pain and suffering and reinvented myself. That is when the shadow self took over from the innocence of my childhood, and until now, it's what I've lived with ever since."

Joe: " You have done some deep and meaningful introspection of your life. I am wondering now how painful it is for you to recall and talk about this event. So, on a scale of one to ten, ten meaning the least painful to remember and one the most painful, where would you consider this past event in your life now?

Alvis thought for a while and answered, "I guess it rates about two on the emotional scale now."

Joe seemed quite taken aback by Alvis's response and asked: "Of the ten things we have discussed in our prior sessions, where do they rate on the scale of one to ten?"

Alvis: " They all rate around two, I guess." Alvis realised at the time that the medications for depression that he was taking may have clouded his judgment, but it was where he felt he was emotionally back then.

Joe contemplated Alvis' reply, for he was mindful of his state of mind: " Do you have any Super?" Joe enquired. " Yes", replied Alvis. Then, to Alvis's surprise, Joe advised, "I suggest you cash it all in, travel the world and root yourself silly. I can do no more for you."

It was thus that Alvis recalled. He ventured forward on the advice of a wiser head than his own and put a smile on many a woman's dial, but it was all in vain. All it did was bring more heartache and sorrow to the adventurer in the long run.

Alvis had let his Keil, his shadow self, have free rein on these con-quests. Still, now he was more aware than ever that it was the inner work with the child that was his priority, and he needed no other distractions in his better state of mind, as he had entered a golden age of being in his dotage. It was therefore crucial for him to be clear-minded and in control, allowing his imagination of the child within to take root in the lotus flower of creative ideas, enabling him to express himself. He began to meditate and recalled a dream he had whilst on the Camino.

It was on a summer night in a village albergue on route to Santiago on his first Camino that Alvis was recalling. He had fallen into a deep sleep and was awakened by the shaking of his bed. He looked down in the twilight to discover three small boys at the base of his bed. They had been tugging at the mattress to wake up the older man.. Alvis, in his semi-dazed state, had responded: "I am not afraid of you. Come up closer so that I can see you more clearly." The boy nearest to him made his way halfway along the side of the bed. He was a beautiful, happy-looking child with enquiring eyes. " What is your name?" The older man enquired. "I am Alvis," said the boy. Right then, Alvis recalled himself at the same age, gazing at an older man in a bed and asking the same question of himself. He was the older man, and the young child brought together over universal time to confront one another. The boy retreated to join the other children, and all three vanished into the night. Alvis then got up and switched the light on; to his surprise, the mattress had moved nearly half a meter from the edge due to the tugging of the little boys.

Alvis had long ago let go of the sadness, isolation and abandonment he felt as a child and in his later years. There had been many an emotional loss, death and disappointment throughout his lifetime. He had learnt to let go, accept whatever transpired on any given day, and overcome the desire for recognition and applause. He had steeled himself to newfound wisdom and a contentment he had never known before. If his books and songs were to be his legacy, then to him now, it didn't mean so much. For he was wise to the fact that all men have their place in the sun for but a brief period in time, and eventually all return to the dust and are soon forgotten. He thought briefly of the mother lode, his mother, for she had appeared to him after her death. He had been in bed at the time, like the visitation of the children. She had stood close to his bed, her eyes fixed on him in a long, lingering gaze. He felt her emotional self enter near his heart. It was as if she were telling him that she was alright now, on the other side of the curtain. As a final gesture, she had an earnest address to the child within, saying, "Be a good boy." The mother lode disappeared into the mist of the night as quickly as she had arrived.

Alvis was thankful that the interviewer had not probed too deeply. Besides his newfound wisdom and freedom, he had no call to express his thoughts now. Instead, he has to recall his state of mind after each Camino.

On his return from the first Camino on the Napoleon route, he busied himself with another house renovation and wrote copious numbers of poems, which he compiled into a book. He was in full flight by then, as egocentricity had regained control. Although he had no new relationship in his life, it did not matter to him at the time, for he was too busy creating. Inspired by his Camino experience, he recorded his first album of songs, wrote and published his first novel, traded on the stock market, and became heavily involved in gambling on derivatives, all while working full-time in business development. The shadow self had complete control; it seemed to be winning. Alvis was surviving on three hours of sleep a night and, on the surface, appeared to be high on something, although that was not the case. It was a matter of months before he crashed and burned one evening, and he had no recourse but to book himself into a rehabilitation hospital once again. It took some five weeks of rest and recuperation before he gained some quality in his life.

He returned to work again, grieving over all the other pursuits save for an idea he had for another book. It began to take shape in his creative mind, and he found a way to have something tangible to look forward to. He had convinced himself that he not only needed to write about love but also to find a new lover. He had tried to have a relationship, but at the time, he wasn't mentally stable enough to give it a proper go. Thus, he planned another journey, relying on his inner intuition to guide him. He was not as fit as he was on the previous Camino, but he proved he could do it by willpower alone. To test his theory, he climbed Westhead overlooking Pittwater in Sydney. It was almost straight up. He climbed with some bushwalker friends. He recalled that halfway up, they discovered an old rope; it was part rotten, like a vine past its use-by date. The lead climber had taken hold of the rope, and Alvis himself, following a similar experience climbing the mast of the ship, followed a meter or so behind. The rope seemed to hold, and all went well, then came some falling rocks. Like when things go smoothly in life, one must always be on the ready for an Achilles' heel. The lead climber called out, looking down, and said, "Rocks." As the rocks came tumbling down, he let go of the cliff and swung out on the rope out of the path of the rock avalanche, looking down to the next climber as he did and repeated aloud, "Rocks." It was the only difficulty he encountered. The climb to the top proved to him that, despite his lack of fitness, he could make it with effort and a will to do another Camino and gather the material for another book.

To bring his book idea to life, he decided to walk the Portuguese Way instead of his usual route. Fate once again intervened, throwing him off course. He had connected with a female friend on Facebook, a medical professional, who promised that if he went to Lisbon to start his Camino, she would show him around. He found himself drifting again, lost in the shadows of his inner self. He let lust replace love, and that craving led him like a lamb to the slaughter. He spent three months chasing shallow pleasures. In the end, he returned home with a broken heart, wiser from the pain and sorrow he had endured. Once again, he went back to rehab; Alvis was a hopeless case, not only because he'd lost his way but also because he didn't even know who he was, which terrified him. He found himself back in the garden with his mother, where he had created a false version of himself. His only escape now was to tap into his childhood creativity, so he decided to walk the French route of the Camino. It was to be the foundation of the book he'd always wanted to write. The story would reflect on his first two Caminos and the lessons learnt during those journeys, sharing both true and fictional stories of his third walk. This set something in motion again- writing another Canino story followed by another album of songs. By then, he was over the Camino, and his focus shifted toward what he could create for others rather than just fulfilling his own desires. Because he had found his inner child's heart, and that was the key to loving- a love he had always been searching for.

There were people in his past life whom he felt he needed to make amends to. He had achieved that with many, but when it came to his own family, that was a different "kettle of fish." The mother of his children had left him after decades of marriage. She had taken his worldly rewards, but that meant little to him ultimately, for it was the deception that gnawed at his conscience. It was the broken heart he had felt at the time. None seemed to understand that. He had told her he was sorry about the breakup, but it did not seem to sink in. He had evaluated some time ago that had he been in her shoes when she left home, he could now honestly say: " There she goes, off with another man… I don't blame her. If I had been in her shoes, knowing what I was like back then, I would have left too."

He had thought a lot about his children, too. There were far too many amendments he needed to make. Thinking about it, he had concluded that the loss of his second eldest son by his hand had shattered their lives. He felt that they all, including the mother of his children, needed someone to blame. It was easy for them to live with the sadness of it all if the father was the ogre. He could live with that and concluded that he was not to blame for the route that his son had chosen.

Focus on the Father Lode.

For a brief moment, he thought about the Father Lode, the one he had turned to when the Mother Lode became too tough to handle. Father Lode had given him little time, caught up in his own world. Alvis realised that he was not unlike him; in fact, he had nearly mirrored his life for a while until the wake-up call arrived. Father Lode had been driven by material success, had creative talent second to none, and drank heavily and smoked like a chimney, living on three hours' sleep a night for years while building his empire. Alvis loved him with all his heart. When he died accidentally under the influence, Alvis felt like a string had been cut inside him. He was already on his way out. The accident just sped up the decline. Sometimes in life, it's better to find closure by handing it all over to God rather than reopening old wounds. Like a chapter in a book, one day Alvis turned the page and began a new chapter in his life. He wrote a song about losing his father. He recorded it for those who suffer the pain of alcoholism. As for love, Alvis was recalling his AA ninth step now: "Made direct amends to such people wherever possible, except when to do so would harm them or others." He could only pray for the repose of the souls of his Father Lode, his Mother Lode, and now his son.

Alvis made his way to the seashore in his mind at dusk. He was feeling the love and the hurt that sprang from deep within. He, thinking of his father, of his mother and his dead son, remembered a poem by a fellow Australian, Jamie Grant, that resonated with where he was at that moment:

Seabirds at sunset skim
Towards the horizon, glassy rim,
The day's pure light grows dim
As we remember them..

The ways of love now seem unfamiliar to him. He was on a learning curve, embracing the heart of the child without completely ignoring his shadow self. He realised he needed to express his creative side through his child; logic and reason told him this. Alvis had concluded that the ego of the shadow self was not necessarily a bad thing, as long as it did not become a self-will run riot. After all, he wouldn't be doing this interview if he had no ego. The shadow self also needed to express its feelings. Alvis's analytical mind could see the wisdom in this, because without ego, there would be no action.

Alvis was reflecting now on his battle with love overwhelmed by lust. He had once mistakenly thought that his betrothed was a prototype of his idea—one created in his image and likeness, like a mirror of the love within him. Eventually, it all turned out to be an illusion. Then came the many love scenes, which appeared like a garden of flowers. Some were vivid in his mind, and he could almost smell their scent to his heart, while others were like those pressed flat between the pages of his life's journey.

Loves reflection.

It was but yesterday that he had walked among the field flowers, It was evening, and the moon appeared to kiss the earth, and everywhere he looked, love and the world responded to him as proudly as the sunset he'd just seen.

All shone in the twilight of his heart's voice, the child within, and he remembered her lips that trembled under the light of the moon. The honeybee was still humming around the lavender. 'And graceful, bittersweet flowers flirted with the colours in the fading light, and there was colour everywhere.

So it was that in everything he could see her image, the image that breathed virtuous psalms to life. And the movement of the flowers in the slight breeze, rolling like a river, was in the stars, in the rolling fields, that brought him back to memories of immortal happiness.

The mood of the scene told Alvis' heart-child how she, in a flowering past, as they had lain by roses, would hold fast to him for her long gaze, which spoke of tender and voluptuous feelings. Oh! Fair love, pure fiery soul, who never wronged me, never once, but I did not see you then as I do now. I did not know the way to drain from fortune's chalice the nectar that comes from a woman's gentle touch. The heart strings, the pure intention of the child's love, can only be measured by.

Yes, Alvis had told the whole story more than once in past writings, in stirring tones, of the loves he shared that joined two souls as one. The murmurs of the flowers, kindred spirit to the wind, and the mild breath of the perfumed that whiffed over the earth, like rain over the plains. And Alvis still thought that he could hear the sweet nothings that his fond nest had created for him, the bright sound of laughter and the childlike voice that echoed back to him, for he had traced her love in the clouds and in that perfume breeze of that fragrant afternoon.

How vividly he remembered the symbols of the saints, those days when he released inspired verses, and there, beneath the sky, amidst the blossoms, they drank in the exhalation of that fragrant afternoon. And the wallflowers of vanilla essence and the cabbage roses, more mournful than a burial, led me to reread the great novel; his child had written whilst in exile, with whisper-less kisses on the moonless nights.

Ah! No longer so, Alvis no longer sits on those brick benches, carpets, in moss, and I will no longer kiss your ivory fingertips, thin and delicate like the aftermath of budded flowers, in evening fading hours. Because I did not know how to love the motions of your silent harmonies, my heart now aches, my spirit flags, and my laughter turns to tears, as I recall my cruel Judas' smile when he betrayed Christ.

As Alvis remembered how he had now freed his captive memories, built a whimsical castle in the air, and leaned over the pond to gaze at his reflection, where he once used to lean, where the moonlight's yellow rays would come to rest. And he believes he still can feel and hear his faith, now more gentle than a prayer, from behind a veil of solace, her divine, stone-softening gaze, which locked him long ago within love's prison. And he could see her dainty feet still, these soft, smooth feet. He thought he had buried them in his hands, and fancied that amid the birds' discourse, he heard it as the heavenly song of the nightingale, a heavenly song of the angel.

Alvis awoke from his dreaming as the studio lights illuminated his soul, and then a passing breeze seemed to carry him away again. He heard the sound of a vibrating voice and momentarily thought it was hers—a metallic voice—and he sniffed her fragrance, that sweet perfume. He had been sleeping in the chair and was awakened by the technician, as the finale of his interview was about to resume.

For only a brief moment, he thought of the sun slipping into its final moments, heard a church bell toll a slow, grave knell in the distance, and wondered, was it for him? He reflected on the sorrow of passionate love and the dying sickness of death that one day would come to claim him. His most profound thought was of an incredible night when darkness might shroud him, who would gather the flowers for his grave and who might close his eyes for the last time.

The interviewer was shuffling with his clipboard, now ready to speak with his guest once more. As Alvis shook off thoughts of loves once had but now lost, and the toll of death's bell, he braced himself again for the moment. He need not dwell on death, for there was still too much living to do, and he reminded himself that times past had more to tell in tears than those now remaining, so he should make the most of the 'present,' the gift of life; as some people called it.

The in-review addresses the child within, and Alvis had to discern whether it was wise to nurse the in-review questions as his logical half-brain would have previously done, or leave it to the truth of the pure wound in his heart —the pure child within to answer them.

Alvis spoke silently to his heart: 'I befriend you, dear one, do not think I love this worldly existence as I once believed I did.' It's been a lifetime since I last felt the blood bloom within my veins, and perhaps the grave will be kinder to me than the life that has spanned most of my years. So I no longer yield to pleasure's lure, for when my time comes, I shall leave this painful world with ease. Oh! Fair child, I long for your merciful gaze, and soon enough I will gaze upon my dying form in silence. Yet you should know that I no longer desire to flee the world and visit its creatures, but I will not forsake you with my sorrow, until the eve of the day you too shall die—die of grief that you no longer live! I can't bear so much, though my bones ache and my energy is drained. I will stay strong again so that you may live, so that you may create within me another sonnet, another song, another story. It is my duty to you to live on; it is you who will have the hour of glory. The ghost of myself, Alvis, will let you take the stage, accept the accolades, and bow to the audience.

So you will not come to nourishment beside the rustic blooms, and need not water the ground with your tears, the ground of piteous weeds. For you shall arise like a seed to flowers to bloom from those beds of flowers within you shall bloom, like rose, and the daffodils you shall grow and flourish in bloom, while the dahlias of despair will weep in the jasmine's arms!

It came to pass that Alvis allowed his child self to answer the remaining questions from the interviewers through the child within.

Interviewer: "Alvis, you've had a long life and have written about it in your stories, poems, and songs. Don't you think you've done enough? Is it not time to let go and seek something else in your twilight years? "

To the surprise of the Interviewer, the children within Alvis stated: " I have only really just begun. In truth, I shall write my heart's desire for my true love and form through that glass darkly the meaning of my heart."

The interviewer then attempted to lay a trap in his questioning to test the genuineness of his guest.

Interviewer: " So Alvis, if you had but one hour to live, were writing a story or a song, what would you do with that remaining hour.

Alvis, from the child within, said:" I would continue writing the story or the song."

It was then that the child within encouraged Alvis to pick up his guitar, and as he headed for the microphone, he decided to take charge by saying to the interviewer, "I wouldn't know how to end my story, so I would now like to close with a song." The interview had no recourse to interrupt proceedings, allowing his guest this honour.

The child spoke quietly to the audience through Alvis, his adult self and asked a simple question: "Does anyone here know what a hack writer is?" He waited a whole for an answer and hearing none, said:" Well, you probably know from experience what it is when someone hacks a computer, or uses a hacksaw blade, right?" The Alvis child laughs aloud; "Well; a hack writer might be considered someone who has produced a large quantity of words that have meaning but lack the heart of the writer, for he may have gained wealth of fame as a consequence of his authorship, but in truth he is a hack producing work primarily for financial gain or to meet deadlines, rather than for artistic expression or passion." "So, I am going to create a song for you now, a song that expresses my feelings, as well as my head and worldly experiences, and how I feel about my book and songs."

Alvis, as he had done with the Santiago song for his child's expression earlier in the programme at the studio, started working on some chords, and with them, the Child found his voice: "This one's called 'Old Bush Hack'."

Well, I am an old bush hack
With a knapsack on my back
I've no work now
No money for my pride.

And I've tried my hand at busking
selling songs and books outback
I've no place to call home
And that's a fact.

So I carry my books
For insurance
CDs of the songs
 that I wrote,

For a dollar or two
I'll sell you the bloom'en lot,
But my backpack and sleeping pack
They are worth their weight in gold,

So I'll not be selling you that.
No, I'll not be selling you that!
Well, I tried my hand at busking
 So many songs I sang

At the country music shows
A one-man band.

There's no money in life
Of a country music man
And authors are a dying breed
As any fool would know.

Oh! It's no stable life
No one to call my own
When loves come
They just as surely go.

So I carry my books
For insurance,
CDs of the songs
that I wrote,

for a dollar or two
I'll sell you the bloom'en lot,
But my backpack and sleeping sack
They are worth their weight in gold,

So, I'll not be selling you that
No, I'll not be selling you that!

Well, I'm an old bush hack.
With a knapsack on my back
I've no work now
No money for my pride.

And I've tried my hand at busking
selling songs and books outback
I've no place to call home
And that's a fact.

So I'm on the frog and toad
 With a knapsack on my back
 I'm heading for some place
 I've never been.

Alvis' child asked his audience to sing along with the chorus verse with him, and they sang in unison. Everything a child could ever hope for. And Alvis looked back, and he made his way from the stage, seeing the big movie screen with the still shot of his book page from his website still on display. Alvis was pleased, as was the child within, as was the shadow self, for he knew with some chance his time would come again.

The crowd left, and the interviewer had a warmer conversation with his newfound hero. He was a fan now, but Alvis was saving none of this for his shadow self. Nor did he consider it to have anything to do with the child. He was a frank, older man, sitting in a chair on a stage —a place he had known all his life since childhood. The difference was that he no longer performed; he was not confined, as he had been in his childhood. He could just be himself, an old man content to be. He stayed in the theatre until the lights went low, fell asleep for a time and woke up in pitch-black darkness. He felt his way along a wall until he found a tiny switch. As luck would have it, he had switched the lights along the footpath to the theatre exit. He was grateful for that, as he was more concerned about damage to his guitar than hurting himself in a fall.

Alvis had plenty of time now to go through the motions of living in the present. He had been thinking that he would muse over it for a while longer before making his next move. For it no longer mattered to write for fame, for money, for glory, or ego. He was now on a new wave, guided by the creative genius of his inner child. He had the choice now to enter the dragon's mouth of the lotus flower of innovative ideas or not. He would simply hand it over and see what emerged in God's good time. He did not have any idea where he was heading, nor what, and he didn't care, for he was free at last to follow the road less travelled or the broad, wide highway. It mattered little either way, for he had no one to impress, had all he needed for a comfortable daily living, and now had a place in the sun he could call his own in his heart.

The coming of age of the child.

Alvis was comfortable in his skin. He did not need anyone else's opinions or advice. He was reminded of his boyhood imaginary friends and superheroes whom he had emulated as a child. First, there was the influence of Dave Crockett. It was before television, and he took to reading books about his hero, gathering historical information wherever he could find it. At the time, there was no TV to turn to, only radio, and the only film at the Saturday Picture Show was the 1955 version of Davy Crockett, King of the Wild Frontier. A year later, in 1956, Davy Crockett and the River Pirates followed. This series and film are known for the catchy theme song, "The Ballad of Davy Crockett."

Dave Crockett was known for killing a bear as a boy by shooting it with a muzzle-loaded rifle; the powder was loaded and rammed down the barrel, and the trigger fired a flintlock, igniting the shot, unlike the latter rifles that load through the breach. In his early years, he wore buckskin tops and trousers, along with moccasins, like the Indians of those pioneering days. Of course, later, when he represented the state of Tennessee in Parliament, he wore neither formal nor casual attire. Later, he was killed in the Battle of the Alamo, which is a key event in the Texas Revolution, where Texan settlers and volunteers fought for independence from Mexico. The battle, which took place from February 23 to March 6, 1836, resulted in the death of all the Texan defenders, including notable figures such as William Travis, James Bowie, and Davy Crockett.

Alvis remembered that Davy Crockett and Jim Bowie were heroes to the kids in the bush during their preteen years. The only local hero they could relate to at the time was Ned Kelly. He was seen as a villain of the worst kind by the conservative faithful. So, we boys had no other option but to read classic comics and biographies of our heroes. Alvis's transformation happened when a remake of the film "Robbery Under Arms" was made in 1957. It was then that we had an Australian villain the kids could secretly admire. But the Hollywood portrayal of The Alamo and Crockett was deeply embedded in our minds when I was just ten. A mate had a replica gun, which he had carved with a red-hot iron, "Old Betsy," in the butt — the heart of Davy Crockett's weapon. Alvis had a Bowie knife with a steel blade, not Sheffield, but made in the USA. The Mother Lode had a fox fur for formal occasions. Fox fur coats and wraps were all the rage for women in the 1950s. Alvis got it into his head to make a coonskin-like cap out of Mother's wrap. Besides, she didn't wear it much. He believed he would get more use out of it as a look-alike Davy Crockett. Alvis laid it out on the bedroom floor with a pair of scissors in hand, ready to cut, when she walked in. It was a tongue-lashing he never forgot.

Movie heroes were his frequent escape, and it wasn't long before, as a teenager, Alvis was imitating Elvis Presley and another hero admired, James Dean, whom he later wrote a song about. When TV cameras became more common, there was a surge in popular serials to watch, and Daniel Boone became the man of the moment, as Dave Crockett faded in folk hero status.

Alvis reflected on how he had abandoned his more conservative values even before he was a teenager. He had no choice but to follow community standards, which were enforced through corporal punishment by the nuns and eventually the brothers at boarding school. Still, he never lost his rebellious streak. He now understands that was part of the reason he went off the rails later in life. The seeds were sown long before his first drink, and the effects of drinking had given him Dutch courage during many events. It was against his nature in his life until he finally crashed and burned, as he had previously mentioned.

Time never stands still, and Alvis was observing his slow acquisition of wisdom, which seemed to come much later in his case than in that of other young men his age. Marriage, the responsibility of a home loan, educating children, and finding his way in the world had caused him to leave behind his childhood self, his heart, and his true soul love, adapting to the demands of respectability, business, and religious ideals. In the end, it was all for nothing, except for the moral values that somehow endured through thick and thin, like scaffolding on a timeworn building.

Alvis was taking it all in, even though he was now free to chase the next right thing to do in his creative life, for the time now remaining before the death knell bell would toll for him, too. He brushed aside that thought. Stay in the now with the 'now' mantra of "Live! Live! Live!" he kept repeating. As he recalled the waves to the shore, he repeated that mantra again and again, repeating it in his head like a drumbeat.

The old adventurer in his "golden years,' as he liked to call them, was, despite his good ear for music, experiencing some hearing loss. He refused to wear hearing aids, accepting the decline as a natural part of ageing, because if he missed a few words, he knew he'd sort it out in the end with a bit of patience. Life, he thought, is a constant challenge, recalling the cataract removal he had a couple of years earlier, when he also found out he had macular degeneration in one eye. Though his back and hips sometimes ached, he didn't have osteoarthritis; his heart remained strong despite many years of alcohol and cigarette use. He appreciated this and felt blessed by his circumstances. Taking pills to control his blood sugar was his only main medication. He had long given up on depression meds and showed no signs of dementia. Alvis felt freer now than he had at any other time in his life.

So it was that Alvis, in his newfound connection with his child's heart's desire, stepped out to forge his way on a new adventure into the unknown. He carried only a small pack this time. Content with just one change of clothes, a small sleeping bag, and limited food and water, he was in his element as he began to climb the first mountain slope in New Zealand after a long absence from the land of the long white cloud.

The reentry of the shadow self.

Alvis reached a peak and gazed across the horizon, taking in the mountain range beyond and the lake below. Feeling pride at his achievement, he rested for a while, unzipping his backpack and pulling out a notepad and pen. He jotted down some lines to remember later. He settled on a couple of quotes from Sir Edmund Hillary from when he first climbed Everest. He had been asked by a reporter why he climbed it. He responded, "Because it's there." Alvis remembered another quote from Hillary: "It's not the mountains we conquer but ourselves." Then he wrote down another remark, recalling from author Greg Child: "Somewhere between the bottom of the climb and the summit is the answer to the mystery of why we climb."

His egocentric shadow self once again tricked the old mountaineer Alvis as he proudly thought of his achievement. The dark spirit had entered his mind, reminding him of how hard he had struggled to reach the summit. Alvis began to believe that it was the strength and stamina of the shadow he needed all along. He could not leave him behind while in action mode. It was not his creative mind now; it was the will of the deceiver he relied on. Of course, ethos was an ally, and he fought to keep his logical mind intact. He felt weak and fell to the ground as the shadow took control. If a passing observer had been there, they would have seen an older man lying on the ground as if having an epileptic fit, which he was not. The dark one had him now fighting his demon. The voice inside had told him that if he gave in to his desires, he could have the wealth of anyone he chose to deceive. He would be given the ability to cheat another out of their wealth and take any man's wife for a lover of his choosing.

Alvis was irritable and discontented, and his fears fuelled his flaws. He was fighting hard now, and the dark spirit tried a different approach. Alvis became angry and yelled out with the venom of a snake at his tormentor. The shadow self then promised him that if he stopped and surrendered, it would bring him a feast fit for a king when he left the mountain. Unable to break Alvis, the shadow tried its last ploy to trap him. As Alvis felt he was about to break free from his dark self, he became utterly exhausted. The demon told him he need not strive at all, to become lazy, and he would grant him all his desires without effort. Alvis resisted, and with iron will and the love he had helped nurture within him, he fought off his faults and once again found freedom.

Soon, he regained his composure, took a sip of water, and ate a bit of his food. Before long, he felt strong again and began making his way along the ridge at the top of the mountain, happy to stroll and watch the sunset, his shadow now behind him, both in spirit and in reality. Alvis had learnt a hard lesson. It was about finding a balance. The evil and corruption that could cause him the most distress. He knew he had to give his ego its due when he needed extra willpower and strength, but he couldn't let it overshadow his self and get carried away, or he would just as surely come undone.

Likewise, he had to learn the same lesson with caring for his pure spirit, as it could also exhaust him in creative pursuits. Alvis understood that peace was only achievable when he let go and allowed his higher power, that spiritual presence in the light, to take control—just as it might take control of the light within him, as well as the darkness within.

A Position of Power

Alvis was contemplating again how position and power shape one's way in life. Success and failure are the opposite sides of the same coin, so to speak, and self-suffering is a quality not always easy to cultivate while maintaining compassion for others. The symbolism of money, position, and power was clear to him — he knew that 'out there in the world' it once was, and he was determined to be part of that world. But now he was not of it — being of the spirit within and the creative self-assurance, he was walking in the presence of his true values, which were clear to him.

He reflected on the myths of his past ambitions and greed, his power and failures, his responsibility and irresponsibility, and realised that his self-worth and longing for love were now more important than ever.

It was his own mythical story that he concluded helped him discover his proper place in the world, his true vocation. He knew now how to respond to society. He could discern right from wrong in all things. Myths had held him back from revealing his true strength, as well as his weaknesses, hiding his truth as much as his hypocrisies, and his sometimes misguided value systems, which lacked understanding of worldly motives. Now, he was coming to grips with his belated acquisition of wisdom. He had now discovered his inner calling, his vocation to accomplish what he was being led to be, expressed through outward action, whether it was raising his inner child into creative action for others or simply tending his garden in a semi-meditative state. Alvis had written extensively on this topic in the past, so as he walked the mountain track, it was more a review of where he stood in living in the spirit. He was now enjoying the mountainous adventure. Walking the path of least resistance, he felt like a younger man in the afternoon of his life, in the afternoon of nature now, for both the sinking sun and his inner soul self were basking in it.

It was fear that had driven him in his former life before he discovered how to tap into his creativity and write books and songs. Before entering the dragon's mouth of fear of what he might find, he was then all shadow self, for it seemed to be the only way he could cope. He had lived based on the unfulfilled demands of his shadow, in a state of continued disturbance and frustration. He had learnt not to form the outward expression of his innermost desires. Although he could make it all happen with his previous half-brained notions of how to live, it took the mastery of his three parts of himself—his child self, his shadow, and his analytical linear brain—in unison to give and get the best from his newfound freedom of living and expressing himself for love of all that made life worth living.

He now understood that peace could only be achieved by letting go of expectations. It comes through surrender to his creator, his higher power of understanding. The child self knew how to express kindness, love, and generosity of spirit just as surely as the shadow self could express anger, selfishness, and those seven deadly flaws in his character that need calming. The child helped with his, as Alvis sang poems that emerged from within him. Music to soothe the savage beast that dwells inside.

Alvis set out on the mountain trail the next morning after finding a hut along the way to sleep in. He felt refreshed after a relatively restful night's sleep, even though he dreamt of many monsters, goddesses, witches, and warlocks. It was not these dreams that troubled him, but instead, such dreams filled his mind with ideas to incorporate into another story.

Introspection on the Way.

He was heading south now, the morning so clear behind him as was his shadow. He stopped for a moment, analysing his child's curiosity, wonder, and genuine emotions. It was what drove him to write and sing songs, he thought. He felt joy in his heart and was happy knowing he had healed his unhealthy wounds through his creative expressions and, without being egocentric, his spontaneous wisdom.

Alvis put away his notebook and, with a quick glance at his own shadow behind him, realised that the epileptic-like fit he had fought with the previous day was driven by repressed desires and a fear that he might not be able to love again. He concluded that he was now close to living and enjoying his previous uncontrolled desire and lustful actions. The idea of "Go to God and not to the women, and you will find the answer to that riddle" came to mind. He knew that the shadow had not completely let go of him and mused that it probably never would, for it still held the ultimate goal of death over life, and one day it would come to this. For now, though, he could not acknowledge its supreme power over feelings.

It was vital for Alvis to keep that ego in check, tapping into it only when necessary, without allowing it to dominate his conscious mind. It was his mature ability to observe within the rationality of his current life situation. He could not be cold-hearted about it, but instead used his knowledge, life experience, ego, and the child's creative nature to build bridges of benefit for himself and others, without question. He believes he would therefore benefit others as well. He was aware of his choices in a conscious way to move with the month. Inspiration would come and go, but he knew now not to tap into every idea, as he didn't necessarily have to act upon them all as he once had.

Alvis took out his notebook and started writing again for future use. He didn't need to come up with another idea for a book or song, nor did he need to worry about what might happen next. He reflected on how he preferred working from home with creativity rather than embarking on adventures, but he hadn't given up the idea of blending creativity into his daily routine. He had noted that he was now inclined to integrate his better self, free from past greed and selfish expectations. He thought about the story of Dr. Jekyll and Mr. Hyde, the struggle between his shadow self and his true self. He also thought of Dr. Fustus selling his soul to Satan's shadow to gain universal knowledge, only to realise that his lack of self-will, fear, and feelings of abandonment in his youth had driven much of his life. He had long masked his life with pursuits of fleshly pleasures, like Dorian Grey in Oscar Wilde's story, who indulged in debauchery and reckless adventures to fuel his desires. The image of a young man of virtue by day was corrupted by night. His alter ego was depicted in a painting hanging on his wall, showing him growing uglier and more decrepit each night, while his real self remained untouched. Dorian Grey ultimately dies, and his body takes on the flaws of his corrupted soul, while the painting reverts to its original, pure form. In a dream, Alvis saw his own image as that of Dorian Grey, but it faded and turned into a mirror reflecting his true self. From bitter experience, he knew he could no longer live a life of deception. He decided that he would struggle to be genuine and keep writing creatively. His child was healing from wounds, and despite personal pain and sorrow, his purpose was to seek worth by helping others.

The old adventurer followed the ridge of the mountain track that led downwards towards the ocean. In the distance, through the valley below, he could see the diamond-like sparkles of the sun's reflection on the water. He would arrive there by nightfall. As he made his way down the mountain to the valley floor, he began to ponder how to approach his life's work, balancing his creative desires, wants, and needs in a way that supports each other, guided by his inner voice. For the first time, he realised that he could harmonise his grounded child, shadow self, and analytical mind to achieve his goals.

The inner child would trust him, but the shadow self, with its cynicism, might react; however, it could be kept in check and used at will. He was already relying on his mind's analysis, which was competing to some extent with his heart's intuition. His child's creativity was therefore vital to maintain a balanced approach to his new life's work. He had to let go of self-protection in favour of self-service, be aware of the triggers in different aspects of his personality that could lead to misguided choices in his relationships. Alvis had broken many hearts over a lifetime, and despite all this, bearing his own dreams shattered, he now had a clear vision of how he could help others with their broken dreams and hearts. He had a lot to work on; that much was clear. The challenge was not so much the goals or tasks he had to achieve, but how to harness his creative child's output, his shapeless shadow self, to make his analytical, ethical, liberal conscious mind interact harmoniously with his makeup.

The man, in the prime of his life, his glorious age, began to consider the world in which he was endeavouring to put his creative child into action once again. He thought of all the suffering and hardships he had been through, all the nights of the soul he had experienced, and he started to assess whether it all had any real benefit to his better self, or for that matter, to others.

Certainly, if he entrusted all his efforts to a higher power, goodness and mercy would come from his connection to others. It now seems, as he reflects on life as good or evil, that the supreme good, which is God, would balance any evil with good or divine purpose. Then he remembered St. Augustine's writing on this matter: "When a thing is corrupted, it is evil because it is, but not just as much, an impairment of good. Where there is no need for the good, there is no evil. Where there is evil, there is a corresponding dimension of the good." Alvis thought that Augustine sees evil, both physical and moral, as a weakening of goodness. It is the opposite of good, like darkness is known through light. Therefore, what is evil must be understood from the nature of good. If suffering is a form of evil, then suffering exists because of good. It can be said that man suffers because of a good he should have shared but was deprived of, or when he was meant to share it with others but did not. This sickness is a poverty of health; loneliness is a poverty of happiness; war is a poverty of peace.

The challenge of accepting the world's ailments — a world torn by conflict that Alvis no longer wanted to be part of but couldn't escape — was his dilemma. If he allowed his creative side to flourish and gave his shadow self some freedom to push the cause forward, then evil might potentially seep in; however, he hoped that good would ultimately prevail, for his intentions were rooted in goodness and love.

The biblical tale of Job's trials came to mind. For Alvis, his descent into darkness resembled Job's suffering, which was biblically justified as evil. He was reflecting on how it happened. The shadow self, the Satan within, had tried to take over Job's innocence, as he had immense faith in his God, his father. The supreme lawgiver had been talking with the evil one, who suggested he could win Job's favour by putting him through trials of suffering. If he succeeded, Job would likely lose faith in God.

The aim of moral order is to demand punishment for wrongdoing. The evil one believes that Jobs' shadow self will win his soul if he suffers enough as a result of his actions. God accepts the challenge because he trusts his faithful servant. Suffering may seem like justified evil. Job, however, rejects the idea that suffering equals punishment. Job's friends accuse him of wrongdoing and suffering as punishment for his immoral deeds. God has allowed this evil to continue. Job recognises that he is innocent of their judgment. However, God permitted an innocent man to suffer by inflicting a form of punishment despite his innocence. It remains a mystery why God allowed this, but Alvis considers God's ways beyond human understanding. He concludes that not all suffering is due to fault and that some suffering is a just punishment. Suffering of an innocent person without guilt, even if they have done no wrong. Despite all his trials, Job did not lose faith in his Higher Power. The gift was that Job regained his wealth and had a new family, living with the knowledge that, despite much evil, good always triumphs in the end.

Alvis thought as he headed towards the seashore that he was not unlike many humans, bitter from early rejection in his life that had overshadowed his soul and pushed him towards power and worldly lure. He decided that because of abandonment, he couldn't grasp love and chose wealth and dominance instead. Yet, his wealth brought him no happiness, and eventually, others who lacked ethics stripped him of his money, power, and status as well.

Avis had written about the myth of it all. The myth of a dark portrayal of life in the material jungle, and he had seen it firsthand in this modern world of business, finance, and politics. He observed it in the shadowy world of his family's manoeuvrings during the inheritance process, the property division after his father's death, and his divorce proceedings. For a past life experience that has been formed in his mind, a symbol of that within us all that reacts to personal disappointment with rage and bitterness—the shadow self, the deception of genuine feelings towards our fellow human beings.

In his mythology, every man is to some extent a myth within himself. It was the pursuit of the symbol of wealth and power, associated with a river of gold, that he saw in his current state. He had once chased this symbol to win the heart of a beautiful maiden, a mythical nymph. In his youth, he envisioned the gold at the bottom of the river waiting for him to claim it, believing he could win the heart of his desire with jewels and riches. Like every man, within his creative reach was his collective psyche—the gold, an image of nature's resource—there for the taking.

Reality has shown that all the striving driven by the will of the shadow Alvis rather than his delicate creative spirit would ultimately not bring tears of joy. Yet, in the depths of heartache and sorrow, he concludes that he does not need to go there for his progress, even though he may have endured ill health to reach those depths. Slvis was now hesitant, not wanting to tempt fate by returning to his old ways of achievement. He knew that such gold could be brought into consciousness and used either for humanity's benefit or its destruction.

For a time, his wounded heart swore off love forever and dedicated all his efforts to chasing goals, but they slipped through his fingers, leaving him miserable and seething with hatred and rage. As a mythic image, his shadow self's ugliness embodies an internal 'quality' that responds to the scornful allure of the damaged female. He now realises that he no longer needs to act on such feelings or abandon his higher values because he has come to understand, in his wiser years, that we cannot force life to give us what we want when we want it. Alvis's soul was once shrunken by his lack of generosity, tolerance, or inner confidence to ignore the teasing of ant nymph. The realisation that we cannot justify all human destructiveness by blaming a harsh and challenging environment. Alvis had learnt that his human character might choose to act or react either with hatred or understanding. Alvis said aloud: "We all face such chances, possibly many times in our lives, and we thus shape our future through them."

Alvis comes to believe that we do not need to turn to any religious philosophy expecting some material reward or a special gift to understand the inner logic of his mind. Such things come from God as they are beyond human comprehension, a mystery of supernatural nature within the universal plan. The lesson he learnt unfolded as a hard knocks lesson. In the myth, his intense craving for wealth and power was a twisted by-product of emotional pain and bitterness. It makes him justify behaviour that disconnects and distorts the truth in his relationships with those he perceives to love. He concluded that it was not wealth that was the root of all evil, but how he used it to vindicate, justify, and compensate in his ability to forgive.

Alvis was now strolling along the seashore, listening to the waves. There was no sign of life or death, just the gentle lapping of water against the shore, and the constant roar of the ocean; it was his only sound. While creativity remained his goal, he was aware that his future achievements involved not only risks and rewards but also responsibility, both internal and external.

The voice of the Mauka, the child within, was craving attention. The wise old adult Alvis gently soothed it, assuring that the pure child could create anything whenever it chose. That he, Alvis, would dedicate his attention to the child's outpourings whenever the creative surge arose. Hearing and understanding this, the pure child felt the older man's love and embraced it fully.

Meanwhile, the shadow self sat within the man's feelings; he would not give in to the urge to control and pour strength into the golden age, so it might once again dominate his life. Alvis acknowledged its presence too but maintained control over it. He was not going to hand over to this dark spirit as he had done most of his life. Alvis was aware of the Keil, the shadow that had been crucial to the man's success in business and the ways of the flesh. However, he knew all too well the chaos Keil could cause if he let it loose. So Alvis, asserting his authority, made it clear to the spirit that he, Alvis, would call on Keil whenever he chose. Only if the egocentric Keil accepted this; otherwise, he would send him back into the darkness where he belonged, even if it meant suffering for the older man.

Alvis, now wise, recalled the aftermath of his lifetime's profound success. It often led to depression, a rise to grand corruption of his spirit, the lies of Keil, the shadow self, which haunted the child Manka. When he took time out to recover, he knew that idleness was the devil's plaything. It came at a cost: focusing on lust instead of love, an insight into a corrupted spirit that Alvis had in the past but lacked the foresight to foresee. He knew too well the temptations of the flesh, being blinded by lust in a demonic mood, risking turning to another's flesh instead of godliness within. He understood the striving for perfection—the battles and hardships to finally gain his God link in love, then the expectation to feel content, fulfilled, and at peace. So often, the opposite happened, and Alvis found this puzzling. He couldn't understand why, having climbed to the top of the mountain, the view proved to be grey, bleak, and devoid of hope. He was now examining it from every corner of his mind—whether for worldly responsibility or the pursuit of material things—so much of what drove him, or what he believed he needed, was to have, win, or gain something. A story that revealed a secret within the human heart. He now knew it wasn't the prize but the struggle that made him feel alive; it was in his creative child-like expression—this offering of love and commitment to the gift that was his greatest reward. 'It is the struggle that makes us feel alive,' he thought, 'which brings out the best in us.'

Alvis was reflecting on the pattern of his former self, having achieved success in the real world with recognition and wealth. Yet, after reaching these heights, everything began to spiral into emotional turmoil, physical illness, and the darkest nights of the soul. It was his imagination of the hero within, this symbol of motivation inside him, that drove him to write songs and novels. He might never have done this if it weren't for the cries of his inner child and the shattering of his egocentric worldview. Alvis realised he needed to endure the hardship of emotional disappointment to fight in worldly terms, even though he felt that nothing of the world mattered to him anymore. He wanted to win the great fight-what was it for? Was it for the power of his impetuous and noble spirit? Or was there any point when there was nothing left to fight for? In peace, his fighting spirit became a serious problem. The armour of faith had, at some point, turned sour. Despite his doubts and frustrations about the slow progress, he knew he had to keep going. It was the Achilles' heel of his motivated spirit that he risked defeat—this inner sense that life no longer held any meaning.

Alvis had indeed achieved his ambitions. It was only then that he realised he belonged to a larger community. It was not his aim to impress others with his shadow self, an egocentric notion, but rather his contribution to the greater good that flowed within him was now his merit. He had to admit that in recent years, he had become more at peace, being more involved in the life of the wider world. He knew this deep down. It was easier with the ego intact most of the time because he had won many of his worldly battles, having already discovered his natural resources, limitations, and responsibilities to others. He could then turn inward and recognise what he had achieved: the use of his talent, with the help of his inner pure spirit, guided by his higher power. Discover what it had all been for, to whom it belonged, and what it served.

Alvis was present with nature as he walked along the ocean shore. He felt a deep connection to the natural world, experiencing a sense of belonging and emotional attachment, part of the whole, with the sand under his feet, the water lapping over his toes, and then receding again. Seagulls swooped and dove with a rhythm he hadn't noticed much before, but they too now felt like part of him.

He recognised an inner interconnectedness with all living things and appeared to genuinely value nature's beauty, diversity, and complexity. As if the God of nature was giving him a sign, a pod of dolphins started to herd a school of fish near the beach. It was a sight to behold, like riders on horseback rounding up cattle and driving them to market. These masters of riding the ocean waves, diving and swooping, had the fish at their mercy, but only briefly to get their fill, then left most of the fish to continue their collective movement.

It seemed to Alvis that God, in His mercy, had given the dolphins the foresight to take only the fish they needed for their survival. He knew that fish in schools, except for dolphins, **can confuse and disorient predators, making it harder for them to single out and attack an individual. He knew that fish in schools can be more efficient at finding food sources, reducing energy expenditure, and making it easier to find a mate, too.**

The beauty of nature—the sky, the sea, and the shore—was all within the adventurer's view. He felt deep inside that he was free, as were all the creatures in his sight. He knew then that all he had to do was connect with the energy of it all, for it was up to him; he was granted that freedom.

Alvis suddenly felt as if he had developed a sense of responsibility and a forward-looking resolve to protect and care for the environment. He saw a plastic bag drifting on a distant wave. Alvis took off his clothes and plunged into the ocean. He swam towards the wave, grabbed the plastic bag, then rode the next wave to shore and put the bag in his knapsack to dispose of later. It was a simple act, but a meaningful deed for the environment: a small step, yet a clear sign of the right course. I must stay alert, he thought. He understood he needed to be aware of whatever was presented to him to do from now on. So, his insight related not only to his inner world but also to the outside world—all he had to do was believe in the process and act accordingly.

Alvis was now thinking of a Russian legend about a peasant who was told a wise man's message: if he ran to the next village on a set day, he would receive a parcel of land if he did just one good deed. On the set day, the peasant ran, did a kind deed upon entering the village, and was given an entitlement to land to call his own. So, he returned to the starting point and was told that he would receive even more land if he completed another task. Although it was near dusk and he was exhausted from running most of the day, the bloke set out again to finish his task. He did just that and ran home again with another deed to go; he was now wealthy in land holdings. However, by nightfall, he collapsed from complete exhaustion.

To Alvis, this exemplified the futility of modern life. He saw, as Solomon did in the Bible, that people gain things but can't truly enjoy them. They work for wealth but then lose it, acquire education yet remain miserable. Whether they gain everything or lose it all, they die like a puff of smoke—here one moment and gone the next. What, then, is the point of living? He understood it like the story in Ecclesiastes, which records a man's search for meaning, his quest for happiness, and his pursuit of reality. Solomon asked, "What is the point of life under the sun"?—a phrase he used twenty-nine times. He had everything—fame, family, fortune, wisdom, women, riches, song, enslaved people, and silver—and yet he was feeling down. He wrote, "I hated life" (2:17), and he expressed feelings of despair (2:20).

Alvis opened his Bible to the passage in Ecclesiastes about Solomon, with the words, "Meaningless! Meaningless! Everything is meaningless" (1:2). He thought he could just as easily say that life is empty, frustrating, and confusing. Still, he couldn't quite understand why. For him, it was like chasing the wind. He had experienced oppression, and no one was there to console him. He had been poor and forgotten for a time; he worked hard, only to see what he gained taken away, and he tried to be righteous but faced ridicule. When he finally regained material success, he couldn't fully enjoy it. Then, just as he gained wisdom, he wasted it away again with foolishness. His investments initially seemed successful, but on another day, they weren't. Like Solomon, work, wisdom, and wealth can all amount to nothing. Why bother working if it only brings pain and grief (2:2 23)? Why be wise if the wise die just like fools (22:15-16)? Why bother acquiring money if we might lose it through some misfortune (5:13-14)?

In examining the Biblical story, Alvis concluded that many human efforts seem pointless, and life offers us much that we simply cannot understand. Solomon wanted his readers to accept that life presents its mysteries: we can't figure out everything; we all face enigmas; our days are filled with frustrations; and life often feels like a riddle. Admittedly, Solomon was pessimistic as he faced reality. He aimed to prevent his readers from relying too much on their efforts and energy. However, this was not his final message. Ecclesiastes does not leave us hopeless and despairing. Yes, at times, life appears like a jigsaw puzzle with missing pieces. Yet, Solomon went further than that. He provided a realistic view of life, acknowledging problems and shortcomings, recognising injustices and uncertainties, but also offering two positive suggestions.

"A man can do nothing better than to eat and drink and find satisfaction in his work" (2:24). "There is nothing better for men than to be happy and do good while they live. That everyone may eat and drink, and find satisfaction in all his toil—this is the gift of God" (3:12–13). "So I saw that there is nothing better for a man than to enjoy his work, because that is his lot" (3:22). "Then I realised that it is good and proper for a man to eat and drink, and to find satisfaction in his toilsome labour under the sun during the few days of life God has given him—for this is his lot" (5:18). "So I commend the enjoyment of life, because nothing is better for a man under the sun than to eat and drink and be glad. Then joy will accompany him in his work all the days of the life God has given him under the sun!" (8:15). "Enjoy life with your partner, whom you love, all the days of this meaningful life that God has given you under the sun, for this is your lot in life" (9:8). "However many years a man may live, let him enjoy them all.… Be happy, young man, while you are young, and let your heart give you joy in the days of your youth" (11:9).

The message here to Alvis, as to any other human, is not hedonism—eat, drink, and be merry because you will soon die. The reality is that to work and to eat are gifts from God for those who please Him (2:26). Solomon reminds us that, despite all life's enigmas and inequities, we should appreciate what God has given us. To be happy in one's work is a gift of God (5:19). As Paul wrote, God "richly provides us with everything for our enjoyment." (1 Tim. 6:17). Solomon had tried everything in his life —pursued and thought of too much pleasure, followed materialistic values, gained wisdom, silver and gold; built great projects, and pursued his artistic interests in song, music and dance, and he had a Herem, too, but it proved all to be folly.

Alvis put away his Bible and reflected deeply on his time as an adventurer on the road. He had moments to stop, meditate, jot down a poem or a song in his notebook, and record his days' activities—what he saw, what he envisioned, the lessons he learned—and rest for a while by the Snafu track towards the beach. When he woke up, night had fallen, the stars shone brightly in the sky, and the moon looked as if it were in the seventh heaven. He knelt to pray and give thanks for his day. He was not lonely or frustrated with his lot. "The man who fears God will avoid all extremes" (7:18). "I know that it will be well for those who fear God, who fear Him openly. It will not be well for the evil man… because he does not fear God" (8:12-13, NASB).

Alvis laid out his sleeping sack, and before drifting off, he acknowledged to himself, "Fear God and keep his commandments, for this is the whole duty of man" (12:13). He was reflecting on Solomon, who tried everything—pleasure, wine, wisdom, building projects, enslaved people, animal husbandry, silver and gold, singers, and a harem (2:1–8). But he had to admit that when he considered it all, "everything was meaningless, a chasing after the wind" (2:11). The secret to life, then, isn't found in possessions. Instead, two keys unlock the door to fulfilment, meaning, and joy: enjoy life and fear God! To fear God means we stand in awe of Him and depend on Him, not ourselves. We recognise that we are human and finite, whereas He is divine and infinite. Alvis was already in a deep sleep. Almost as soon as he laid his head on the pile of clothing, he sat up again, using his clothes as a pillow.

The old adventurer was up early and on the bush track, making his way towards the end of his wanderings. He had new pursuits to fulfil his heart's desires. He carried a neutrality in his being, like that of a pure child. He walked with a creative mind, aiming to benefit others, into the morning sun, with his shadow following behind him in its proper place. He was of a clear mind and open to the mercy of God's will.

In these twilight years, he pondered how he might find fulfilment in a cottage by engaging in more hobbies, connecting even more deeply with nature, whether that meant tending to his garden, spending time with loved ones, or pursuing personal interests. He knows that he will continue to maintain his physical and mental health and well-being. Ultimately, he realised that he would find purpose in sharing his wisdom and experiences with younger generations and contributing to his community.

There would be no kudos in his intent, for it was more than just writing books as a catalyst to his wellbeing, or singing a few of his songs; it had more to do with the benefit of those who were willing to listen to the older man.

So it was that the older man, having nothing better to do, sat with his guitar and began to sing to a group of young people. He had seen it throughout his lifetime, and things were moving faster for him now. The facts were still there, but truth can come in a disguise. He was determined to get that point across to them:

A silhouette is cast upon a wall,
the shadow self of life is fading fast,
and yesteryears don't matter any more,
at least that's how it seems in growing old.

And now we're in the time of AI,
old ways are fading quickly by,
the things we once believed in don't seem to matter much today.

Do we live a life of fake news?
Is it up to you and me to take a stand, or will truth prevail in
the end? What will you sacrifice for truth?

Still, you've got to stand tall before the fall.
Stay free to live life after all,
blossom like a flower, or a leaf on a tree,
before it turns to autumn of its change.

We do get a second chance after all,
to be born again, like the seed of an oak,
grows to be the most enormous tree of all,
a place for the singing of the birds.

Do we just live a life of fake news?
Is it up to you and me to take a stand,
or will the truth prevail in the end?
What will you sacrifice for truth?

There is no mandate or law for truth,
to be free of spirit or in chains,
for the desolation road is wide,
and the narrow gate is harder in the end.

The morning star is rising once again,
old Lucifer has your name in his book,
and he wants you to follow his path to the end,
promising a return to glory hour.

A silhouette is cast upon a wall,
the shadow self of life is fading fast,
and yesteryears don't matter anymore,
at least that's how it seems in growing old.

Do we live a life of fake news?
Is it up to you and me to make a stand?
Or will the truth prevail in the end?

What will you sacrifice for the truth?

In Matthew 19:16-22, a wealthy young man asks Jesus what he must do to inherit eternal life. Jesus tells him to keep the commandments, and the man claims to have obeyed them all. Jesus then challenges him to sell all his possessions, give the money to those in need, and follow Him. The man, unable to part with his wealth, walks away sad, highlighting the difficulty of prioritising God over material possessions. This passage emphasises that true discipleship involves not just outward obedience but also a radical surrender of self and worldly attachments.

The rich young man's question shows a desire for eternal life and a belief that it can be earned through good works. However, his question also reveals a misunderstanding of the nature of God and salvation, which is not earned but freely given. Jesus initially points to the commandments as a way to life. He emphasises the importance of moral conduct but also shows that simply keeping the commandments is not enough for salvation. It demonstrates that true righteousness comes from a relationship with God, not just outward rule-following.

Jesus's challenge to sell all his possessions and follow him exposes the man's attachment to his wealth and his inability to surrender to God truly. Such a requirement demonstrates that worldly possessions can be a barrier to following Christ. The young man's sadness highlights the challenge of relinquishing worldly attachments and embracing a life of radical discipleship. It highlights the cost of following Jesus and the necessity of a complete surrender of oneself.

The surrender of the pure inner child, the sacrifice involved in overcoming the will of the shadow self and the analytical mind in genuine authenticity, is the priority that God desires us to serve Him humbly. It is a tough challenge for everyone to rise to, dear reader. This small work, through my self-analysis, may assist you on your path to salvation, as I hope it does for me as well.

Doug McPhillips, poet, singer, songwriter, and author, commenced his journey of discovery over a decade ago after life-changing experiences.

The many tracks he has traversed through the Northern Hemisphere and down under in Australia and New Zealand have contributed to the facts and beliefs about the spiritual essence of this novel.

Doug has written twenty-five books, many of which relate to personal spiritual growth and belief.

Doug is an adventurer who divides his time between family and friends, his creative pursuits, and those who benefit most from his efforts and experience.

25/7/25

www.ingramcontent.com/pod-product-compliance
Lightning Source LLC
Chambersburg PA
CBHW040233170726
48295CB00014B/909